Dear Reader:

Thank you for picking up the third book in the *Santa Claus: Super Spy* series. As you may remember, the money paid to buy the first two Super Spy books was put toward the cost of adopting a child.

I am thrilled to announce the adoption of our son, Jonah Sanford Jacobson. He is the greatest joy my wife and I have ever known. (You can see a picture of him near the end of this book.)

I had a lot of fun writing *The Case of the Colorado Cowboy*, and I hope you enjoy it as much as I do.

Sincerely,

Ryan Jacobson

www.operationadoption.com

Super Spy
Secret Code

1 = A	10 = J	19 = S
2 = B	11 = K	20 = T
3 = C	12 = L	21 = U
4 = D	13 = M	22 = V
5 = E	14 = N	23 = W
6 = F	15 = O	24 = X
7 = G	16 = P	25 = Y
8 = H	17 = Q	26 = Z
9 = I	18 = R	

Can you solve this secret message from Santa Claus?

The first letter is filled in for you.

M __ __ __   __ __ __   __ __ __ __
13-15-13-19   1-14-4   4-1-4-19

__ __ __   __ __ __ __ __ __ .
1-18-5   8-5-18-15-5-19

Santa Claus:
SUPER SPY

The Case of the
Colorado Cowboy

by Ryan Jacobson
Illustrated by Erica Belkholm

Maggie,
Yee-haw! Keep reading!

LAKE 7 CREATIVE
Mora, Minnesota

RJ

2/11

For Mom and Dad,
forever my heroes.

Special thanks to Nikki Dorau, James and Cheri Jacobson, Rachel Knight, Tricia Nissen, Karla Schiller and Emily Sykes.

Cover illustration colored by Elizabeth Hurley.

ISBN-10: 0-9774122-2-9
ISBN-13: 978-0-9774122-2-8

1 2 3 4 5 6 10 09 08 07 06 05

Printed in the United States of America by Sentinel Printing, Saint Cloud, MN.

November 2007

Super Notes from Super Readers

"Your books are AWESOME!"

Blake, Age 8

"I love your books. They are so exciting."

Beth, Age 12

"Your book was so good. None of my family wanted to stop reading it."

Grace, Age 8

"Your books are cool. I hope someday I can meet you."

Kailey, Age 8

"I love your book. So far it is the best book ever."

McKenzie, Age 9

*Ryan would love to hear from you! You can write to him on the Internet at **www.santaclaussuperspy.com**.*

What Is a Super Spy?

Santa Claus has a secret. He's a Super Spy. He chooses boys and girls across the country. Together they protect the world from danger, using their Super Spy watches and gadget belts.

Now Santa and his top agents, Paul Jenkins and Emily Swanson, visit the state of Colorado to solve a puzzling mystery.

Contents

Santa Claus: SUPER SPY

1

Family Vacation

Car rides are boring, thought Paul Jenkins. His family was on vacation, driving through the midwest part of the United States. Paul had been sitting in the back seat of his parents' car for days. Worse yet, he was trapped with his brother: Matt the Brat.

Paul tried to get along with his younger sibling. After all, Santa Claus had chosen Paul to be a Super Spy, and Super Spies were supposed to be kind. But Matt made it hard.

"Stop touching me," he whined.

"I'm not," said Paul. "I'm just sitting here."

1

"You're touching my side of the seat. Mom!"

Paul's mom and dad had listened to the boys argue for most of the week. His parents had been nice. Then they had gotten mad. Then they talked about turning around and going home. Their latest tactic was simply to ignore it.

"Mom," screamed Matt.

"Will you please be quiet?" said Paul. "Look, I'm moving over."

The nine-year-old boy squished farther into his corner of the car. Matt smiled to himself, as if to say, "I win." Then he went back to looking at his book.

He's always trying to be better than me. He always wants to get me in trouble, thought Paul. *I wish I could tell Mom and Dad I'm a Super Spy. They'd know I'm the good one, not Matt.*

Paul remembered his two adventures with Emily Swanson, his partner. They helped Santa Claus stop

Jack Frost from freezing Florida. And they saved Delaware from a giant dinosaur. After that mission, Santa sent a message to every Super Spy, telling them how brave Paul and Emily were. Paul wished Santa had sent the message to his parents too.

"How are you doing back there?" asked his dad.

"Fine," Paul answered.

But that wasn't true. His mom and dad were good people, but their idea of fun was different than his. They liked to visit museums and factories. Paul preferred toy stores and amusement parks. He also liked animals. Mountain lions, bighorn sheep, elk and bears could all be found in Colorado. So far, Paul hadn't seen any of them.

He kept complaining in his mind, until his dad said, "We're here, kids."

Paul looked up and gasped. He thanked his parents for a wonderful surprise.

They were parked in front of a tiny field. Cowboys, horses and trailers were all around them. Directly ahead, Paul spotted a fenced-in area where a horse galloped to and fro. Shiny, silver bleacher seats flanked the field on its left and its right.

A pretty cowgirl smiled at Paul's family. "Come on in," she said. "The arena may look small, but we've got the best cowboys in the world here."

An enormous banner hung above the cowgirl's large, tan hat. It read, "Welcome to the Rodeo."

WELCOME TO THE RODEO

RODEO TICKETS 10$

2
Three Cowboys

Most boys and girls Paul's age had heroes. For some it was a great football player. For others it was a talented singer or actor—but not for Paul. He loved rodeos, and his favorite cowboy was the world's biggest rodeo star: Carter Collins.

Carter was only a few years younger than Paul's dad, so Paul couldn't help comparing them. Carter was short, while Mr. Jenkins was tall. Carter looked tough in his boots, jeans, red shirt and white hat. Paul's dad was an odd sight in his bright, flowery shirt and his pants that didn't match. Carter had a big smile. Mr. Jenkins' thick mustache hid a tiny mouth.

And, of course, Carter was a brave, heroic cowboy. He lassoed cows. He rode wild horses. He even sat atop the backs of big, mean bulls. He usually won first prize in every event he entered. Paul's dad was great, but he was no hero. In fact, Paul didn't think his dad had ever won first prize in anything.

The young Super Spy remembered the many rodeos he'd seen on television. His thoughts turned to his other favorite cowboys: Wyatt Downs and Don Reynolds. They almost always finished second or third, but they never beat Carter.

Paul believed Wyatt looked old for a cowboy. His hair was gray, and his stomach kept getting bigger. Wyatt once said on TV that he dreamed of winning the National Rodeo Championship. But Carter finished ahead of him every year.

Don, on the other hand, was one of the youngest cowboys. Paul had read an article about him. It said that Don was never happy with second place. In fact, Don told reporters that he wanted to win, and he was ready to do almost anything to make it happen.

As Paul thought about the three cowboys, he squeaked with excitement. He followed his family toward their seats, and he checked his rodeo program. He searched through the names and smiled to himself. Carter, Wyatt and Don were all on the day's schedule.

*****

I'm tired of being second best, thought the villain. *I'm as good as he is. I'm as good as any of them. But it won't be long now. After today, I will be the best. I'll be number one!*

The villain laughed a cruel laugh.

Santa Claus:
SUPER SPY

3
A New Friend

Paul and his family were early. The rodeo wouldn't begin for more than an hour. They found their seats in the middle of the bleachers, about half-way up. Paul looked onto the field, and he decided that these were the best seats anyone could get.

Now what? he asked himself.

As if reading Paul's mind, his dad answered. "Maybe you and Matt should try to get a few cowboy autographs."

"Really?" Paul nearly fell out of his seat.

"Yes, really," said his dad.

Matt the Brat almost ruined it. "I don't want to go," shrieked the boy. "I want popcorn!"

Paul frowned. He wouldn't let Matt spoil his fun, not today.

"Can I go without him?" begged the young Super Spy.

Matt held his breath. Then he screamed. Then he held his breath. Then, once again, he screamed.

Mrs. Jenkins had heard enough. "You stop that right now, or you can watch this rodeo from the car."

Paul almost laughed, but he swallowed hard. He didn't want to get in trouble too.

His dad gave him a quick glance and said, "Yes, you can go. But stay out of trouble."

Paul didn't need to be told twice. He jumped out of his seat and weaved his way down the aisle. He dashed toward the cowboys' trailers, their little homes on wheels.

It was easy to spot Carter. Paul could see the line of fans waiting to meet him. He ran around the fenced area to the back of the field, where most of the trailers were. He took his place at the end of the line and counted nearly 20 people in front of him. He heard a few fans hop into line behind him too.

The Super Spy couldn't see Carter any more. But he heard someone in front yelling, "Hurry, I don't have all day!"

At least, Paul said to himself, *the line is moving quickly. I'll be up there in no time.*

His thoughts were interrupted by the voice of someone standing in line behind him. "Nice watch."

It sounded like Paul's best friend, Emily. The boy spun around, expecting to see her.

Instead he looked into the green eyes of a girl he didn't know. She smiled at him and pointed to her own wrist. She was wearing a Super Spy watch too.

4

Gizmo the Horse

"You're a Super Spy?" whispered Paul.

"Yes. My name is Cassidy Tomms, but my friends call me Cassie."

"I'm Paul Jenkins."

"I know," said the girl. "You're the one who captured Jack Frost, and you helped Santa stop a real-live dinosaur."

Paul smiled shyly. Then he asked, "How did you become a Super Spy?"

"The same way as you, I suppose. I got a Super Spy watch for Christmas, and Santa started sending

13

me secret messages."

"Have you gone on any missions?" asked Paul.

"Of course," she answered. "I'm a very important Super Spy."

Paul liked his new friend. He could tell her all of his secrets. He shared his stories, and she told a few tales too. All the while, the line brought them closer to Carter Collins. But bad news was waiting.

"That's all the time I have today," declared Carter. He turned and left.

"Oh, rats," said Cassie. "Carter's my favorite cowboy. He's the best."

Paul's smile dropped. Tears began to well in his eyes. He didn't want Cassie to see him cry, so he looked away.

"Hey," said the girl, "that's Carter's horse Gizmo over there. Do you want to pet it?"

Paul saw the brown steed tied to a trailer.

Meeting Gizmo isn't as exciting as meeting Carter, he thought. *But it is the next best thing.*

The two approached the saddled horse. For a second, Paul thought someone was standing behind Gizmo. He saw a crooked black hat and a thick, dark moustache. The shadowy figure looked a lot like Don Reynolds. But when Paul looked again, Don was gone.

Cassie and Paul introduced themselves to Gizmo. They took turns petting the horse and telling it how beautiful it was. Its red and brown saddle matched the horse perfectly.

Paul dreamed of riding Gizmo. He imagined sitting on the horse, galloping across the field. He wrapped his hand around a strap that dangled from the saddle, admiring its smooth texture.

"Keep petting him," Cassie said to Paul. "I'll take a picture."

15

The girl pulled a tiny camera out of her pocket. She aimed it at Gizmo and Paul, ready to snap a shot, but then she suggested another idea. "Give Gizmo a pat on the side. Maybe you'll get him to look at you. That would make a better picture."

Paul patted the horse, and all of a sudden Gizmo let out a **NAY!** It bucked and jumped wildly. Paul couldn't step back; his hand was stuck inside the strap.

The horse continued to bounce and buck, neighing loudly and stomping its hooves. It jerked its head, snapping the rope that had held it to the trailer. The horse bolted toward the fence, but Paul's hand was still stuck. Gizmo was dragging him away.

16

5
A Cowboy Rescue

Paul wasn't sure what had happened. A second ago, he'd been holding the strap in his left hand and petting the horse with his right. Now Gizmo was running, and Paul's hand was caught. He was being dragged through grass and dirt.

He felt the strap cutting into his wrist. His shoulder ached as his body pulled against his arm. With Gizmo's every stride, Paul bounced again and again onto the hard, rough ground. The Super Spy reached forward with his right hand, trying to find something to grab. He'd have to pull himself up before he got hurt. Paul blindly felt the saddle for anything to grasp. He found nothing. He was helpless.

Paul's entire body hurt, and he thought he might pass out. He closed his eyes. That's when he heard someone shout, "Whoa, there! Whoa!"

Paul peeked just as Carter Collins' white hat flew off his head. The cowboy wrapped his arms around the horse's neck. His big, tan boots dug into the ground. Paul felt the tension in his arm ease as Carter slowed the horse to a stop.

The Super Spy untangled his left hand. Then he slumped to the ground. He closed his eyes again, just for a second.

When he opened them, it was like a dream. Carter Collins, Wyatt Downs and Don Reynolds all stood over him. Cassie was there too.

"Are you okay?" she asked.

Before Paul could answer, Carter broke in. "What did you do to Gizmo?"

"I didn't... I don't... I'm not sure."

Carter took a deep breath, as if he were about to say something very loud and very cruel. Wyatt stopped him.

"Looky here, Carter," he said. "Somebody put a spur under Gizmo's saddle." He held a tiny, spiked wheel for Carter to see.

"That's a dirty trick," said Don. "You put a spur like that under a horse's saddle, and it pokes him. That'll make almost any horse crazy. Yes, sir, that's a dirty trick. I like it."

Carter wheeled toward the children. "Where did that spur come from?"

"We didn't do it," said Paul. "Honest."

Cassie added, "We were just petting Gizmo, and he ran away."

"Somebody put it there!" hollered the cowboy.

"Let's just be thankful no one was hurt," Wyatt replied.

Another thought occurred to Carter. "One of you cowboys did it, so I'd lose the roping contest."

"That's just plain dumb," answered Don. "I don't need to cheat to beat the likes of you."

Paul wasn't so sure. He'd seen Don standing next to Gizmo—at least he thought he had. And even if it hadn't been Don, something odd was going on. It looked as if Paul and Cassie had stumbled onto a Super Spy case.

6
H-E-L-P

The cowboys continued arguing and shouting at one another. None of them noticed Paul and Cassie slip away.

When the Super Spies could no longer hear the angry men, Cassie asked, "What do you think?"

"I think Don did it," Paul replied.

"He doesn't seem too friendly," added Cassie.

"No, he doesn't, and I saw him standing next to Gizmo. At least I think I did."

Cassie considered Paul's answer. "What should we do now?"

Both children fell silent as they tried to come up with a plan. Finally Cassie said, "I wish Santa were here. He'd know what to do. And he'd be really proud of us for finding our own mission."

Paul agreed.

"Maybe we should call him," suggested Cassie. "Do you know how?"

The young boy thought for a moment. "I guess I've never tried, but I wonder if we can do it with our Super Spy watches."

"Right," said Cassie. "Maybe we can send a code to the North Pole."

Paul added, "I bet we can make a code word using the numbers on my watch."

"Good idea. What code word should we send?"

"How about H-E-L-P?" suggested Paul.

As he adjusted the time on his watch, Paul thought to himself, *H is 8. E is 5. L is 12 and*

P is 16. I'll set the time to eight o'clock, five minutes, twelve seconds and...

"Oh, no!" exclaimed Paul.

"What's wrong?"

"The last letter—I mean number—there's nowhere to put it. The watch only has hours, minutes and seconds."

But as Paul explained his problem, the strangest thing happened. A fourth number appeared on his watch. He looked at his wrist just in time to notice. His watch read 8:05:12:16. Then the numbers vanished, and his watch returned to normal.

"Wait a second," Paul said to Cassie. "I think it worked."

"How do you know?" she asked.

"I don't. We'll have to wait and see if Santa comes. But for now I'd better check in with my mom and dad."

Paul led Cassie to the arena seats where his parents were sitting. Before he could say a word, his mom blurted out, "What happened to you? You're a mess!"

Paul remembered his unexpected ride with Gizmo, but he couldn't tell his mom that story. Instead he answered, "We were just horsing around."

Cassie giggled.

"We?" asked Paul's dad. "Who's your friend?"

"This is Cassie. Is it okay if I watch the rodeo with her?"

Paul's mom and dad glanced at each other and nodded their okays.

"I guess that's fine," Mr. Jenkins told his son. "But come back as soon as the rodeo's over."

"I will." Paul replied, as he and Cassie started down the bleacher stairs. They were eager to begin searching for clues.

As the two children stepped off the bleachers, Cassie asked, "Do you think they like me?"

"Who?"

"Your parents, silly," she said.

Before Paul could respond, he rammed headfirst into a large, round man. The old-timer was dressed like a cowboy from head to toe. He was wearing tall, black boots and an enormous, red hat. His long, white beard curled just above his belly button. His chubby, red cheeks looked like two tomatoes. Paul had bumped into the leader of the Super Spies: Santa Claus.

"Hi, Paul," came a familiar voice from behind the jolly old man.

The boy peeked around Santa's wide frame, and he smiled his biggest smile. Santa had brought Emily Swanson with him.

7
Reunion

Paul stepped toward Emily and hugged her. He hadn't seen her in weeks.

"I never get used to riding in Santa's super fast sleigh," she said. "We were at my house a minute ago, and now we're here."

Cassie chimed in. "Who is she?"

"And who is she?" echoed Emily.

"Ho! Ho! Ho!" laughed Santa Claus. "Emily, meet Cassie. Cassie, this is Emily. Both of you are Super Spies."

The girls smiled politely and shook hands.

"All right," boomed Santa, "let's hear about why you called us."

Paul and Cassie shared their news of the day's strange events, while Santa and Emily listened to their tale. When the two Super Spies had finished, Santa nodded. "You were right to call for help. Someone may be trying to hurt Carter Collins. For now, protecting him is our top mission."

The arena speakers squawked. "Good afternoon, ladies and gentlemen, boys and girls. Welcome to Denver, the capital of Colorado and the state's largest city. And welcome to the Colorado Rodeo. It's beautiful here by the Rocky Mountains. They call Denver the "Mile-High City" because we're a mile above level ground. We're almost ready to start, but before we do, please listen to these announcements..."

Santa turned to Paul. "What's the first event?"

"The lasso contest," he replied. "It's called calf roping. Each cowboy has to lasso a calf and tie three of its legs together. Whoever does it the fastest is the winner."

"Right," added Cassie, "but the calf's legs have to stay tied for six seconds. If the legs come loose, the cowboy loses."

"Is Carter in that event?" asked the old man.

"Of course," Paul answered. "He's in almost all the events."

"Then we'd better find him quickly," said Santa, "before he gets hurt."

He led his three Super Spies toward the fence's gate. Paul realized that if they walked through that gate, they'd be on the wide dirt field where the cowboys competed.

The Super Spies strolled past a dozen wranglers who were in line for the contest.

"It's a good thing they have a security guard to keep people off the field," said Paul.

One of the cowboys overheard him and began to laugh. "You mean old Clifford? Look closely. He's asleep."

Paul gave the guard a second look, and he realized the cowboy was right.

"Yes, sir," the man continued. "Clifford has slept through every Colorado rodeo I've ever been to."

Paul smiled and thanked the wrangler, as the Super Spies continued their search.

"Keep a lookout for Carter," Santa said. "We have to find him before—"

Again the arena speakers blared. "Ladies and gentlemen, put your hands together for our first roper: Carter Collins!"

"Oh, no," cried Paul. "We're too late."

8
Calf Roping

Paul spotted Carter on the field. He was riding his horse, chasing a 200-pound calf. Santa and the children watched as Carter closed in on the calf, then threw his lasso around it.

Gizmo slid to a stop. Carter pulled the rope tightly, and the calf fell to the ground. The cowboy jumped off his horse, grabbed the calf and plopped it onto its back. He hurriedly tied three of the calf's legs together and jumped away from the animal.

"What amazing speed," hollered the announcer. "If that young cow doesn't get loose in six seconds,

33

it'll be hard to beat Carter today."

But just as the words were uttered, the calf's legs came free. It hopped off the ground and stared at the cowboy blankly.

"Oh, darn," said the announcer. "Carter has been disqualified from this event. Next time, someone should show him how to tie a pigging string."

The crowd laughed at the announcer's joke, but Carter didn't. He stormed to his rope and picked it up. After taking a close look at it, he grunted. Then he marched off the field.

Paul and Emily were waiting to greet him. "Are you okay?" asked Paul.

"Oh, it's you kids again," snapped the cowboy. "What do you want?"

Paul corrected him. "This is a different friend. Her name is Emily."

"You're all the same to me," Carter sneered. "Now, if you don't mind, I'm busy."

"Is there something we can do to help?" Emily offered.

"Unless you can tell me who cut my rope, no!"

Santa Claus and Cassie joined them. "You think someone cut it?" asked Santa.

"Here," said Carter, "see for yourself." He held up the broken ends of his rope. "If it had snapped on its own, it would look torn and uneven. But this cut is perfect and straight. Someone sliced it just enough so the calf could break free."

"Why would anyone do that?" asked Cassie.

"To make sure I'd lose," replied Carter, "and to embarrass me. Now if you'll excuse me..." With that, Carter stalked away.

"That confirms it," Santa said to his Super Spies. "Something is wrong here."

"At least he didn't get hurt," noted Emily.

"Not yet," said Santa. "But if we don't put a stop to this soon, someone will."

9

A Cowgirl and a Clown

"I'd better go and check in with my parents," said Cassie. "Is that okay?"

"Of course," replied Santa. "Catch up with us as soon as you can."

"I will. I want to be the one who solves this case." She turned and jogged toward the seats.

"As for the rest of us, it's time to get started." The jolly old man assigned tasks to both of his Super Spies. He asked Emily to check the area. She'd watch and listen for clues.

Paul was to follow Don Reynolds. If Don were

37

behind all of this trouble, Paul was going to catch him in the act.

Santa Claus chose to stay near Carter in order to keep him safe. "Good luck, Super Spies," he said. "If you need help, use your secret watches to call me."

*****

Paul couldn't find Don, and he had looked everywhere. He had even checked the bathrooms, but there was no sign of the man. The young Super Spy was about to call Santa for help when he heard shouting in the distance.

"Why are you always on my case?" It was Don Reynolds. Paul was sure of it.

He must be arguing with Carter again. Those two are always at it, thought Paul. But it wasn't Carter who answered. In fact, it wasn't a man's voice at all.

"Because all you care about is winning," screamed a woman.

38

The shouting continued as Paul crept toward the loud pair. He peeked around the corner. Don was standing face to face with a cowgirl.

"I can't do this any more," he yelled.

"Good, because I'm late for my event," replied the beautiful woman. She turned and marched into her trailer. Don retreated in the opposite direction.

As Paul ducked to avoid being seen, he noticed a small sign on the trailer. It read, "Nikki Coleman." Don Reynolds had been arguing with the country's top cowgirl.

*****

Emily watched and listened. She wasn't sure what kind of clue she would find. But she was certain she'd find something. She snuck from cowboy to cowboy, weaving her way between crowds of people. She didn't notice anything unusual, though. The cowboys were all preparing for the next event.

"I hate all of them," a voice suddenly whispered from behind her. Emily turned and saw a clown less than five feet away.

Clowns were supposed to be happy and fun, and they made people laugh—but not this one. His white and red makeup was smudged all over his face. His checkered shirt was nearly as dirty as his ripped and ragged jeans. His cowboy hat looked as if a parade of horses had trotted over it. Worst of all, the clown smelled like spoiled milk and rotten eggs.

"I'm sorry, sir," said Emily. "Were you talking to me?"

"Oh, no, no, no," answered the clown. "I was talking to myself."

"Good," she countered. "I'm not supposed to talk to strangers."

"An excellent rule, a very fine rule," the clown stammered.

Emily started to walk away, but she didn't want to go. The clown could hold the clue she had hoped to find.

"Do you know what rodeo clowns do?" he asked.

Emily stopped in her tracks, but she didn't respond. She just listened.

"We risk our lives for these cowboys every day. When a giant bull bucks them off its back, who jumps to the rescue? I do. Who do you think gets chased, bumped and bruised? Me."

"And that makes you mad?" the girl asked.

"Nope, that's just part of the job," said the ugly clown.

"Then why do you hate all of them? I mean, isn't that what you said earlier?" Emily didn't think it was possible, but the clown's face became even scarier.

He stepped toward her and leaned down. "What did you say your name was, little girl?"

Emily glanced at her watch. "Oh, my, look at the time. Santa is—I mean, my mom and dad are probably getting worried. Goodbye."

She turned and ran as fast as she could.

10
Barrel Racing

Paul followed Don to the edge of the field, where the barrel races were about to begin. Carter was there, watching, and so was Santa Claus. Nikki Coleman sat atop a horse, waiting for her turn.

As excitement filled the air, Paul realized that Don was staring at Nikki. It was as if Don knew something no one else did.

The young Super Spy glanced back toward the trailers. He spotted Emily running toward him. It seemed that everyone was gathering for this race. Paul wondered if that were reason to worry.

43

The race began. Nikki's horse darted forward. In seconds, it was around the first barrel and speeding toward the second. That's when things went bad.

Nikki's horse bumped the second barrel, and there was a sudden, loud **BOOM!** The barrel exploded, scaring the horse. It started bucking wildly.

Without thinking, Paul sprang into action. He bolted past the security guard, still asleep in his chair. He raced onto the field, along with Santa and Emily. Paul saw Don running toward Nikki too, but they were all too late. The horse gave a violent buck. Nikki flew off the saddle and landed with a **THUD**.

Santa was the first to reach her. He checked her over and said, "She's out cold, but she's breathing. Stay with her. I'll get a doctor."

"There's no time," Don interrupted. "I'll take her to one."

"We shouldn't move her," said Santa. But Don hoisted her into his arms and carried her toward the nearby doctor's tent.

"This is very strange," noted the old man. "I'd better go with him." He hurried away, leaving Paul and Emily alone.

It was then that Paul remembered where they were. The duo was standing in the middle of the field. Hundreds of shocked fans—including Paul's parents—were staring at them.

"It wasn't smart of me to run out here," said Paul. "How am I going to explain this?"

11

Angry Dad

Paul and Emily hurried off the field. Behind them, Paul heard the speaker announce, "Please remain in your seats. Everything is under control."

Unfortunately for Paul, his dad didn't listen. Paul could see Mr. Jenkins marching down the steps, straight toward him. Carter Collins watched as the scene unfolded. Cassie also arrived in time to see Mr. Jenkins begin asking Paul questions.

"What's going on?" said Paul's dad. "What were you doing on the field?"

"I was, well, you see…" Paul stammered. "It's

kind of hard to explain."

"You'd better try," answered Mr. Jenkins, "or you may be grounded for the rest of your life!"

"Aw, give the poor kid a break," interrupted Carter. "He was only trying to help."

"Sir," said Mr. Jenkins, "this is between my son and me. Please mind your own business."

Paul thought it strange to see his dad arguing with his hero—especially since they were arguing about him. He only wished his dad saw things the way Carter did.

Mr. Jenkins turned his attention back to Paul. "Well, what's going on?"

Paul considered how to answer. Super Spies never lied to their parents, but Paul knew his dad would not believe the truth.

"There's a man," admitted Paul. "He needed help today. So my friends and I were helping him.

We were with him when the cowgirl got hurt. That's why we ran onto the field."

"Where is this man?" asked Mr. Jenkins.

"I'm right here," said a jolly voice. Santa Claus had returned in the nick of time.

It's a good thing he's dressed like a cowboy, thought Paul. *Dad will believe he is one.*

"Is my son helping you?" asked Mr. Jenkins.

"Yes, he is."

"Was he on the field for that reason?"

"He was," said the old man.

Paul saw his dad relax. Mr. Jenkins was clearly glad to learn that his son wasn't getting into trouble.

"Do you still need his help?" his father asked.

"Only if it's all right with you," Santa answered.

Paul knew that, normally, Mr. Jenkins would not allow his son to be with a stranger. But there was something special about the old man. Paul could sense Santa's goodness and warmth. He was pretty sure his dad could too.

"I guess that's fine," Mr. Jenkins decided. "But try to keep him off the field."

"I will certainly do my best," promised Santa.

Mr. Jenkins waved at his son and reminded him to behave before starting back the way he'd come.

"Thanks, Dad," Paul called.

His father smiled, waved again, and then he disappeared into a crowd of rodeo fans.

As the young Super Spy turned to thank Santa, he noticed Carter hurrying away. It was time for the next event.

*****

This isn't working, thought the villain. *I won't be the best until I get rid of him. Perhaps it will take more work. But when I'm finished today, I will be number one. And he'll be nothing at all!*

12
Hold on, Santa

"It's time for us to get back to the mission," Santa told his Super Spies. "The saddle bronc riding event is next. I'm going to enter it."

"What?" cried the children.

"My job is to keep Carter safe. The best way to do that is to stay close to him. He's in the event, so I'll be able to watch for trouble."

"That makes sense," said Cassie.

"But what if you get hurt?" asked Paul. "Saddle bronc riding is dangerous. You have to ride a wild horse, and it'll try to buck you off. Most cowboys can't even stay on for eight seconds."

"I'll be careful," promised the jolly old man. He smiled at the children. Then he made his way toward the field.

"Wait," Cassie shouted after him. "I know lots about saddle bronc riding. Maybe I can give you some tips."

Paul watched his new friend follow Santa into a tiny, fenced area. She spoke with him as he climbed onto a wild horse.

That horse will start bucking as soon as the gate is opened, Paul thought.

"Ladies and gentlemen," blared the arena speakers, "Carter Collins was our next rider. But we have a new contestant taking his turn. Carter has agreed to ride after this cowboy is finished."

Paul scanned the area, but he didn't see Don anywhere. Emily pointed at the rodeo clown sneaking around the trailers and at Wyatt Downs stomping toward the action. He looked as if he might be angry about something, although Paul couldn't be sure.

The gate swung open. Santa's mean-looking, black-and-white-spotted horse bounded onto the field. It bucked, jumped and ran. At every turn, Santa bounced into the air. But he never let go of the saddle, so he didn't fall.

One second passed. Then two. Then three.

The horse continued to leap madly to its left and its right. Santa started to slide along the horse's back. In fact, it appeared that the whole saddle was moving with him.

Emily asked Paul, "Is the saddle supposed to be loose like that?"

"No," he answered, "someone untied it!"

Four seconds. Five seconds.

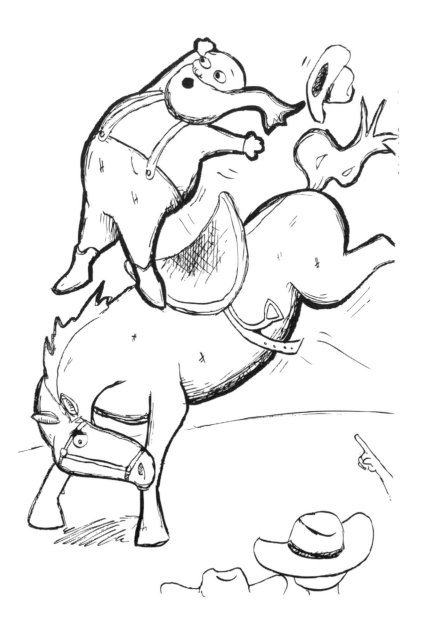

Suddenly Santa flew into the air, along with his saddle. It seemed as if he floated for a moment. Then he crashed to the ground with a **CRACK!**

Paul saw the Super Spy captain grab his left leg. The old man weakly sat up, before closing his eyes and collapsing back to the ground. Santa Claus had passed out.

Santa Claus:
SUPER SPY

13
The Suspects

Paul, Emily and Cassie were inside the big, clean, white tent. Doctors and nurses hurried about as the children stood beside Santa's bed. Slowly, he opened his eyes.

He tried to get up but grimaced in pain. His leg was broken. It was wrapped from his toes to the top of his knee in a thick, white cast.

"I thought you were going to be careful," said Paul.

The old man looked up, and he grinned. "I was careful. But I didn't expect the saddle to be loose."

Paul's smile faded. "It wasn't loose. Someone untied it."

Santa Claus sighed. "That makes sense. When I entered the event, I rode the horse that would have been Carter's. The villain must have thought it was his and sabotaged it."

"Somebody was trying to hurt Carter again," noted Emily.

"I believe so," replied Santa. "The question is, who?"

"Don Reynolds," said Paul.

"You may be right," Santa agreed. "But let's consider the other suspects as well."

"Like who?" asked Cassie.

"Think about what you saw before I was hurt. I got into the saddle that was meant for Carter. The person who untied it would have been angry. Did you see anyone who looked angry?"

59

"I saw Wyatt Downs," said Emily. "He was mad about something."

Santa added, "Don and Wyatt both have reasons for hurting Carter. They want to win the rodeo."

"That's a bad reason to hurt someone," said Emily.

"Is there ever a good reason?" wondered Santa.

Paul chimed in. "I'm not sure about something. Someone put a spur in Gizmo's saddle. Then someone cut Carter's rope. And now someone untied the saddle. Those were all tricks against Carter."

Santa nodded, as Paul continued. "What about the barrel racing bomb? Nikki got hurt, and Carter wasn't even in that event."

"That's a good point," remarked Santa. "Why would someone hurt her, if Carter were the target?"

"It makes me think Wyatt didn't do it," said Paul. "He wouldn't win by hurting Nikki."

"What about Don?" asked Emily. "How would it help him?"

"I'm not sure," Paul admitted. "But I saw them arguing. Maybe he did it to get even with her."

"Maybe he did. But I have another idea," offered Emily. "I think the clown might have done it. He told me he doesn't like cowboys or cowgirls."

Santa, Paul and Cassie considered what Emily had said. At last Santa told her, "Yes, the clown could be our villain."

At that moment, a surprise visitor walked in on the secret meeting, his big black hat ducking into the tent. It was Don Reynolds. He started toward the other end of the shelter, where Nikki Coleman was resting. But he saw the Super Spies and stopped.

"There's something I want to tell you," said the cowboy. "I confess. I did it."

14
Don Tells the Truth

"What did you say?" asked Santa Claus.

"I said I did it," replied Don. "I cut Carter's rope before the calf roping event."

"How could you?" asked Emily. "That's terrible."

"I hate getting second place. I wanted to win, so I cheated. Now I know it was wrong. I don't care who wins or loses. People have gotten hurt."

"I'll say," said Paul. "Look what you did to Sant— I mean, this cowboy."

"What are you talking about?"

Emily glared at Don. "You untied the saddle,

62

and he broke his leg because of it."

The cowboy looked stunned. "I didn't untie any saddles."

"You just told us you did it," said Cassie.

"Right, I did do it. I cut Carter's rope."

"But you didn't untie the saddle?" Santa asked.

Don shook his head, "No."

"What about the spur in Gizmo's saddle?"

"I didn't do that neither."

"And the bomb that hurt Nikki?"

Don turned suddenly angry. "I would never hurt her!" he shouted. "We're in love!" He stormed away from the Super Spies, toward the area where Nikki was resting. The quartet of heroes was speechless.

At last, Santa broke the silence. "I believe him. I think we can take him off our list."

"I do too," added Emily. "That leaves Wyatt and the clown."

"Correct," replied Santa. "Paul, I want you to find Wyatt. Ask him what he knows about this. Cassie, I'd like you to talk with the rodeo clown."

Both children eagerly agreed.

"But that's not all," he continued. "This is too dangerous to handle alone. I want each of you to choose an adult to help you. Choose wisely. You need someone who is honest, kind and brave."

"I'll ask my mom," said Cassie.

"A very smart choice," replied Santa.

"I know who I'll pick too," said Paul. He ran out of the tent without saying another word.

Cassie followed, shouting, "Wait for me!"

Emily watched the duo leave. Then she turned to Santa. "What about me? What can I do?"

"I need you to stay here. We have an equally important task. Together, you and I are going to solve this mystery."

15
Carter Gets Mad

Cassie was alone. She told Santa she'd ask her mom for help, but Cassie knew her mom wouldn't understand what she was doing. Worse yet, she knew her mom would not approve.

All by herself, she crept into the rodeo clown's trailer. Cassie was afraid, but she had a job to do. She only hoped that she wouldn't run into trouble. She glanced behind herself one last time. Then she closed the door, disappearing inside.

*****

65

It's time for my final plan, thought the villain. *This will take care of him once and for all. In a few minutes, I'll become the best. He'll be nothing more than a memory.*

*****

Paul felt nervous as he approached Carter. He had considered asking his dad for help, but he decided that Carter was a better choice. After all, Carter was a famous cowboy.

The star athlete was preparing for the bull-riding event when Paul interrupted. "Excuse me."

"You again?" snapped the cowboy. "What is it this time?"

"I was wondering," said Paul. "Have you noticed that someone is trying to hurt you?"

Carter smiled, although Paul was sure the cowboy didn't find it funny. "In fact, I have," he said.

Paul continued. "I'd like you to help me catch

the person who's doing it."

"You? You're going to catch the bad guy?"

"With your help, yes," answered Paul.

"That's a good one," chuckled Carter. "You're just a kid. How will you figure out who's doing it?"

"I already know," replied Paul. "Or rather, I think I do."

Carter stopped laughing. A hint of anger flashed across his face. "Who?"

"Well, Wyatt Downs is one of—"

Carter didn't wait to hear the rest. He darted toward Wyatt's trailer.

"Downs," he yelled. "Get out here, now!"

Wyatt opened his trailer door and peeked outside. "What's all the fuss, Carter?"

The angry cowboy grabbed Wyatt. He pulled the gray-haired man out of his trailer and threw him to the ground.

"You cheater," hollered Carter, "you tried to hurt me. Now I'm going to hurt you!"

"Carter, wait!" shouted Paul. But it was no use. Carter wouldn't listen, and he was about to do something very, very bad.

16
Mrs. Karla Tomms

"How are we going to solve the mystery?" Emily asked Santa.

"By considering all of the clues," he replied. "The questions we need to answer are how and why? How was each attack done and for what reason?"

"That's going to take a lot of thinking," said Emily.

"Yes, it will," Santa agreed.

Before they could begin, a new visitor walked into the tent. Santa and Emily smiled at the short, stout woman with long, dark hair.

"Hello," she said, "I'm Karla Tomms. I'm looking for my daughter, Cassie. Someone told me she may be in here."

Santa flashed Emily a worried look. "When was the last time you saw her?" he asked.

"Not since the rodeo began," answered Cassie's mother.

Santa pulled Emily close to him and whispered, "She went to see the clown. Go find her."

Emily nodded politely to Karla. "It was nice to meet you." Then she ran out the door.

"Mrs. Tomms," said Santa, "please allow me to explain everything."

*****

Ten minutes passed, then fifteen. Carter and Wyatt continued to argue.

Carter kept telling Wyatt, "You did it!"

Wyatt kept saying, "No, I didn't!"

Paul wondered how long this could go on. But at least they weren't punching each other yet. *I hope Cassie is having better luck than I am,* thought the young Super Spy.

As if hearing her name, Cassie appeared. She was frantic and out of breath. "The rodeo clown," she told Paul. "He's the one."

Carter and Wyatt stopped arguing. They listened as Cassie continued. "He did it, and he's getting away. Paul, you have to stop him."

"Where is he?" asked the boy.

"He's on the field. Go catch him."

"But my dad said..." Paul started to tell her.

"You can't worry about that. You have to go onto the field and get the clown!"

"You're right," Paul decided. "Carter, will you help me?"

"You bet I will," he answered. "Let's go."

With that, Carter and Paul raced onto the rodeo field.

*****

"Something you said troubles me," remarked Santa Claus.

"Oh, what was that?" replied Karla Tomms.

"You mentioned that you haven't seen Cassie since the rodeo started."

"Yes, that's right," Karla answered.

"She told me she checked in with you after the calf-roping event."

Karla thought for a moment. "That's odd," she noted. "Why would Cassie lie?"

"I'm not sure," admitted Santa Claus. But a new idea formed inside his head, and it frightened him.

17
Running with the Bull

Paul and Carter rushed past the security guard, snoring loudly in his chair. They opened the gate and sprinted ahead too quickly. They were almost to the center of the field before they discovered it was a trap.

The crowd of fans gasped, and Paul knew he was going to be in trouble. Worse yet, the clown wasn't even there.

People in the audience began yelling, "What are you doing?" and "Get out of there!" It was then that Paul saw it. A giant, 2,000-pound bull was loose. It was running straight toward them. Its sharp, white horns were aimed at their stomachs.

"I'm getting out of here," whispered Carter. "You're on your own."

"But you're an adult," cried Paul. "You're supposed to help me."

"You picked the wrong adult, kid. Good luck." Carter dashed away, leaping over the fence to safety.

Escaping would not be as simple for Paul. He knew his only hope was to run, but he wasn't as fast as Carter. If the bull caught him, it would stick him with its horns. Or it would trample him. Either way, Paul would definitely get hurt.

He heard the speaker yell, "Oh, no, Carter Collins has run off! Where is our rodeo clown? He'd get the bull to chase him instead!"

As Paul raced in circles, the giant animal drew closer. The boy was scared, but his thoughts became clear. *I sure have bad luck today,* Paul said to himself. He dodged the bull's lunge, wheeled to his left and kept running. *When you take out the trick Don Reynolds pulled, everything else has gone against me instead of Carter.*

Suddenly, it all started to make sense.

When Gizmo ran wild, it wasn't Carter who got dragged. It was me. When the bomb exploded, Nikki was hurt. But that was just to lure me onto the field, so I'd get in trouble. My dad was even going to ground me, until Santa talked him out of it. Then, after Santa helped me, he got his leg broken. And now I'm being hunted by a dangerous bull.

Paul realized the horrible truth. *Carter wasn't the target of these attacks. I was!*

He had finally solved the mystery. There was just one person who could have done it all. One person was with him when he met Gizmo. One person disappeared long enough to set the bomb. One person was close enough to Santa's wild horse to untie its saddle. And one person had led him into this final trap.

Cassie, Paul realized. *She's the villain!*

But what could he do about it? He was trapped on the field, with a bull just a few steps behind.

Again the speaker blared. "Is there anyone brave enough to help that poor boy?"

Paul saw a man with a mustache dart in front of the bull. *What a relief,* he thought. *Don Reynolds is here to save me.*

Paul noticed that Don was wearing a bright, flowery shirt and pants that didn't match. Then Paul saw that the brave man trying to rescue him wasn't Don Reynolds at all.

"Dad?" the boy shouted.

"Run, son," replied Mr. Jenkins. "Run to safety!"

Paul reached the fence and jumped to the other side, landing in front of a bleacher full of fans. He turned and saw the bull hurrying after his father. But, like Carter, Mr. Jenkins ran faster than Paul did. He dodged the bull's attack and dove over the nearby fence.

The bull huffed and puffed in anger. The crowd cheered. Everyone was safe.

18
Cheers and Boos

"What were you thinking?" yelled Mr. Jenkins.

"Dad, I—" Paul stopped. His father wasn't talking to him.

"That was my son out there. And you left him!"

Carter Collins did not reply.

"You're supposed to be a cowboy. You're supposed to be a hero!"

"He's a coward," shouted a fan from the stands.

"Boo," hollered another.

The entire crowd joined in, booing the cowboy they had once cheered.

It was too much for Carter to take. He hurried back to his trailer without saying a word.

Paul rushed to his dad and hugged him hard. "You saved my life. You're a hero. You're my hero."

"I'm just glad you're all right, Paul," Mr. Jenkins told him. It was then that they noticed everyone cheering. The audience clapped and shouted for Paul's dad.

"The applause are well earned," said a warm, soft voice. "You're quite brave."

Paul and his father turned to see Santa walking toward them on crutches.

"Mr. Jenkins, allow me to introduce myself. My name is Santa Claus."

Mr. Jenkins' mouth dropped open.

Another figure rushed onto the scene and hugged Paul. "I'm glad you're okay," said Cassie. "I thought the bull was going to get you."

Paul did not return the hug. He simply asked, "Why did you do it?"

"Do what?" she shot back defensively.

"Why did you try to hurt me?"

"What are you talking about? I'm a Super Spy. I would never try to hurt you."

"Actually," said Santa, "your mother and I had the very same idea."

"My mother?" Cassie noticed Karla standing behind Santa.

"No," said the girl, "you're wrong. It's not me. It's that rodeo clown. He—"

"Cassidy Ann Tomms," shouted Karla, "I didn't raise you to be a liar."

Cassie began to cry. "You don't understand. None of you do. I'm tired of being just another Super Spy. I want to be the best. I thought that, if Paul was hurt, I'd get my chance."

"You're right about one thing," answered Santa. "I don't understand. Why do some people find it so important to be the best at everything? Everyone is good at something, but no one is good at everything."

Cassie looked down. She appeared unable meet Santa's gaze.

"Besides," he added, "it would take more than Paul getting hurt for you to become the best."

"I know," she replied. "That's why I had Paul call you. I was going to solve this case to impress you. I was going to make you think the clown was guilty. But then it all fell apart, and I had to hurt you before you figured it out."

"I'm sorry this happened," Cassie's mom told the group. "This isn't like her. This isn't who she is."

"Yes," Santa assured her. "Cassie is a good person at heart." The old man turned his attention to the young girl. "I won't be able to use you as a Super Spy any more. Your watch will be a normal watch now."

He looked back toward Karla. "I trust you'll take care of the rest."

"I will," responded Cassie's mom. "She'll be cleaning the house from top to bottom for a year."

Santa nodded. "Then that settles that."

Karla left, pulling Cassie with her. Paul couldn't help but wonder if he'd ever see her again. But his thoughts quickly turned to another Super Spy.

"Hey," he said. "Where's Emily?"

19
Real Heroes

Santa, Paul and Mr. Jenkins hurried to the rodeo clown's trailer.

"I hope they're in here," said Paul, as Santa pushed open the door.

They looked inside and were shocked by what they found. The rodeo clown and Emily were tied together, back to back. Their mouths were covered with gags, so they couldn't talk. But both appeared to be unhurt.

Paul pulled the gag off Emily's mouth. She blurted out, "Paul, you have to do something.

86

Cassie's the bad guy... I mean girl. She's trying to hurt you!"

"It's all right," he answered. "We already know. We solved the case."

"You did?" said Emily. "That's a relief."

"Yes, it really is," added the clown, after Mr. Jenkins removed his gag. "Now, will someone please untie us?"

*****

As the rodeo ended, Paul said his goodbyes to Emily and Santa.

"I'm a little disappointed in you," Santa Claus admitted to him.

"Why? What did I do wrong?"

"I told you to choose an adult to help you—one who was honest, kind and brave."

Paul frowned. "I guess I didn't choose very well."

"No," said Santa, "you didn't. You chose a stranger. You picked your hero because of the things he did on television, not because of the things that really matter."

"I'll do better next time," Paul promised.

"Ho! Ho! Ho!" laughed Santa. "I'm very glad to hear it."

"Speaking of parents," noted Paul, "what are we going to do about my dad? He knows my secret."

Santa winked. "I think we can trust him."

Paul grinned and nodded. He turned and hugged Emily, his Super Spy partner.

"Goodbye, Paul," said Santa Claus. "I'll be seeing you again soon. In the meantime, I need to find a Super Spy to replace Cassie."

Santa took Emily by the hand. The case was closed, but there was a hint of sadness on the old man's face. It was the last thing Paul noticed before his teammates disappeared out the front gate.

*****

Paul rushed to the arena seats to find his family. He was surprised by how happy he felt to see all of them—even his brother. He smiled at his parents. And he realized that, for the first time since the trip began, he was looking forward to the car ride. After all, it was a chance to be with his parents, and Mr. and Mrs. Jenkins were the two most wonderful people Paul knew.

Bonus Drawing

In the first version of this story, Paul and Carter were going to discover that the rodeo clown was the bad guy. But then Ryan got the idea that Cassie could be the villain, and that seemed like a bigger surprise. So he changed the story.

Super Spy State Challenge

Test your Super Spy knowledge with these questions about the state of Colorado. If you get stumped, you can find the answers using the page numbers provided.

1. In what part of the United States is Colorado located? (Page 1)

2. Name two animals commonly found in Colorado. (Page 3)

3. What is the largest city in Colorado? (Page 30)

4. What is the capital of Colorado? (Page 30)

5. True or false? Denver is near the Appalachian Mountains. (Page 30)

6. True or false? Denver is called the "Mile-High City" because it is located a mile above level ground. (Page 30)

BONUS: True or false? There is a place where you can be touching Colorado and three other states at the same time.

Got 'em all? Check your answers at the website **www.lake7creative.com/answers.html**.

Visit the Super Spy Website:
www.SantaClausSuperSpy.com

Check out all of the fun activities you can do when you visit Kids' Corner at the *Santa Claus: Super Spy* website:

- Join the Super Spy Fan Club.
- Solve more Super Spy codes.
- Read what people are saying about the books.
- Take the Kids' Poll and send your book ideas.
- Write author Ryan Jacobson a message.
- Create your own Super Spy adventure.

*Be sure to get your parents' permission
before you visit the site.*

Get the Complete Collection of Super Spy Books

*Santa Claus: Super Spy:
The Case of the Florida Freeze*

*Santa Claus: Super Spy:
The Case of the Delaware Dinosaur*

*Santa Claus: Super Spy:
The Case of the Colorado Cowboy*

Order your books at
www.santaclaussuperspy.com

Coming Soon!

Read the following sample
chapter from this exciting
adventure, coming in 2008!

www.lake7creative.com

Following is a preview chapter from the upcoming book Lost in the Wild. *The book will be available in 2008. Visit www.lake7creative.com for more information.*

3
THUNDERSTORM

Thunder boomed. The skies opened. Rain poured onto the two children.

Kate peered through the downpour and realized that they were in trouble. Their canoe was in the middle of an unknown lake, and she could no longer see the shore.

A bolt of lightning brightened the black sky, and panic swept through the Manning girl.

Brandon stood in a frenzy. "We have to get off the lake," he cried. "That lightning could kill us!"

"Brandon, sit down," shouted Kate. "You're rocking the boat! We could tip—"

She tried to finish her sentence, but water filled

her lungs. The boat had rolled over. She was in the lake, and so was her brother.

Her life jacket kept her afloat, as waves slapped her face. "Brandon!" she yelled. She listened for his reply but heard only the roars of water and wind.

She cried his name again. She couldn't see him, and she couldn't hear him. To make matters worse, she had lost sight of the canoe as well.

Never mind the stupid boat, she told herself. *I have to find Brandon.*

The teenaged girl continued her frantic search for the 12-year-old boy.

He's so annoying, she thought. *But I don't want to lose him. This is all my fault, and I don't want to lose him.*

For several long minutes, she searched the murky waters. Brandon was nowhere to be found. Kate felt herself tiring, and her survival instincts awakened. She had to believe Brandon already made it to land. Now, she needed to do the same.

Kate calmed herself, took a deep breath and closed her eyes. She tried to picture what she had seen before the storm began. She tried to remember which shoreline was nearest.

She opened her eyes and turned to her right. *This way, I think.*

Kate slowly and steadily began kicking her legs, pushing herself forward.

Too much time passed. The girl began to wonder if she had chosen the wrong direction.

Her muscles ached.

She couldn't last much longer.

The shape of trees suddenly appeared through the dark rain. Land was just a few feet ahead. Kate pedaled her legs with all of her might. She didn't stop until her knees scraped a mixture of sand and rock beneath her.

She'd made it.

She crawled out of the lake, safely onto dry land. Then she glanced behind her, toward the lake. She hoped to see Brandon coming out of the water too. But no one else was there.

More tired than she'd ever felt before, Kate collapsed into the mud and grass that surrounded the beach. She closed her eyes. Her last thoughts were again of Brandon, as she fell fast asleep.

Bear illustration by David Hemenway (www.davidhemenway.com)

Illustration by Shane Nitzsche

Here's a sneak peek from
a "super" book coming in 2009!

www.lake7creative.com

About the Author

Ryan Jacobson loves to write. He would write all day and all night if he could! In fact, Ryan has been writing stories since he was 16 years old.

Ryan says, "If you want to be a good writer, you should read books and write as often as you can."

Ryan lives in Mora, Minnesota, with his wife Lora, their adopted son Jonah and their dog Boo.

ATTENTION EDUCATORS:

Schedule a guest appearance by author Ryan Jacobson at your school, book fair or special event.

Ryan is an experienced presenter who will lead a fun, interactive and informative discussion about the process of creating a book.

For more information, visit Ryan's website at **www.RyanJacobsonOnline.com**.